PETER RABBIT™ STORYTIME

TALES FROM BEATRIX POTTER

VOLUME THREE

F. WARNE & Co

FREDERICK WARNE
Published by the Penguin Group
Penguin Books Ltd, 80 Strand, London WC2R 0RL, England
Penguin Young Readers Group, 375 Hudson Street, New York, New York 10014, USA
Penguin Books Australia Ltd, 250 Camberwell Road, Camberwell, Victoria 3124, Australia
Canada, India, New Zealand, South Africa

www.peterrabbit.com

First published by Frederick Warne 2005
3 5 7 9 10 8 6 4 2

Printed and bound in Malaysia

Contents

The Story of Miss Moppet

❋

The Tale of Tom Kitten

❋

The Tale of Jemima Puddle-Duck

❋

The Tale of Johnny Town-Mouse

❋

The Tale of the Pie and The Patty-Pan

THE STORY OF MISS MOPPET

1906

About This Book

The Story of Miss Moppet was the second book to be published as a fold-out concertina (alongside *The Story of A Fierce Bad Rabbit*), in time for Christmas 1906. Moppet is Tom Kitten's sister, and the simple story about her exploits with a cheeky mouse is intended for very young children. Beatrix Potter did not want to upset her young audience unduly, writing on the draft for one picture, "She should catch him by the tail – less unpleasant." All ends happily in this delightful story, however.

The book was reprinted in a standard format in 1916 to please the bookshops, and listed at the end of the series of Peter Rabbit books with the other three titles for very young children, *The Story of A Fierce Bad Rabbit,* and *Appley Dapply's* and *Cecily Parsley's Nursery Rhymes.*

THIS is a Pussy called Miss Moppet, she thinks she has heard a mouse!

This is the Mouse peeping out behind the cupboard, and making fun of Miss Moppet. He is not afraid of a kitten.

This is Miss Moppet jumping just too late; she misses the Mouse and hits her own head.

She thinks it is a very hard cupboard!

The Mouse watches Miss Moppet from the top of the cupboard.

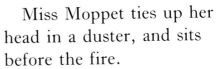

Miss Moppet ties up her head in a duster, and sits before the fire.

The Mouse thinks she is looking very ill. He comes sliding down the bell-pull.

Miss Moppet looks worse and worse. The Mouse comes a little nearer.

Miss Moppet holds her poor head in her paws, and looks at him through a hole in the duster. The Mouse comes *very* close.

And then all of a sudden—Miss Moppet jumps upon the Mouse!

And because the Mouse has teased Miss Moppet—Miss Moppet thinks she will tease the Mouse; which is not at all nice of Miss Moppet.

She ties him up in the duster, and tosses it about like a ball.

But she forgot about that hole in the duster; and when she untied it —there was no Mouse!

He has wriggled out and run away; and he is dancing a jig on the top of the cupboard!

THE END

THE TALE OF
TOM KITTEN

1907

ABOUT THIS BOOK

By the time Beatrix Potter started writing *The Tale of Tom Kitten*, she had owned Hill Top farm, in the Lake District village of Sawrey, for a year. The expansion of the farmhouse was finished, and Beatrix was enthusiastically planning her cottage garden. She could not completely desert her property for writing, and both house and garden feature in the story. Mrs. Tabitha Twitchit leads her children up the path to Hill Top's front door, while inside we see its staircase and bedrooms. The kittens romp through the garden's flowers to jump up on the wall overlooking Sawrey, and the ducks march across the farmyard.

Beatrix used the same kitten as a model for both Miss Moppet and Tom. "It is very young and pretty and a most fearful pickle." She dedicated this story to "all Pickles – especially to those that get upon my garden wall."

ONCE upon a time there were three little kittens, and their names were Mittens, Tom Kitten, and Moppet.

They had dear little fur coats of their own; and they tumbled about the doorstep and played in the dust.

But one day their mother—Mrs. Tabitha Twitchit—expected friends to tea; so she fetched the kittens indoors, to wash and dress them, before the fine company arrived.

First she scrubbed their faces (this one is Moppet).

Then she brushed their fur (this one is Mittens).

Then she combed their tails and whiskers (this is Tom Kitten).

Tom was very naughty, and he scratched.

Mrs. Tabitha dressed Moppet and Mittens in clean pinafores and tuckers; and then she took all sorts of elegant uncomfortable clothes out of a chest of drawers, in order to dress up her son Thomas.

Tom Kitten was very fat, and he had grown; several buttons burst off. His mother sewed them on again.

When the three kittens were ready, Mrs. Tabitha unwisely turned them out into the garden, to be out of the way while she made hot buttered toast.

"Now keep your frocks clean, children! You must walk on your hind legs. Keep away from the dirty ash-pit, and from Sally Henny Penny, and from the pig-stye and the Puddle-ducks."

Moppet and Mittens walked down the garden path unsteadily. Presently they trod upon their pinafores and fell on their noses. When they stood up there were several green smears!

"Let us climb up the rockery, and sit on the garden wall," said Moppet.

They turned their pinafores back to front, and went up with a skip and a jump; Moppet's white tucker fell down into the road.

Tom Kitten was quite unable to jump when walking upon his hind legs in trousers. He came up the rockery by degrees, breaking the ferns, and shedding buttons right and left.

He was all in pieces when he reached the top of the wall.

Moppet and Mittens tried to pull him together; his hat fell off, and the rest of his buttons burst.

While they were in difficulties, there was a pit pat paddle pat! and the three Puddle-ducks came along the hard high road, marching one behind the other and doing the goose step— pit pat paddle pat! Pit pat waddle pat!

They stopped and stood in a row, and stared up at the kittens. They had very small eyes and looked surprised.

Then the two duck-birds, Rebeccah and Jemima Puddle-duck, picked up the hat and tucker and put them on.

Mittens laughed so that she fell off the wall. Moppet and Tom descended after her; the pinafores and all the rest of Tom's clothes came off on the way down.

"Come! Mr. Drake Puddle-duck," said Moppet—"Come and help us to dress him! Come and button up Tom!"

Mr. Drake Puddle-duck advanced in a slow sideways manner, and picked up the various articles.

But he put them on *himself!* They fitted him even worse than Tom Kitten.

"It's a very fine morning!" said Mr. Drake Puddle-duck.

And he and Jemima and Rebeccah Puddle-duck set off up the road, keeping step— pit pat, paddle pat! Pit pat, waddle pat!

Then Tabitha Twitchit came down the garden and found her kittens on the wall with no clothes on.

She pulled them off the wall, smacked them, and took them back to the house.

"My friends will arrive in a minute, and you are not fit to be seen; I am affronted," said Mrs. Tabitha Twitchit.

She sent them upstairs; and I am sorry to say she told her friends that they were in bed with the measles; which was not true.

Quite the contrary; they were not in bed: *not* in the least.

Somehow there were very extraordinary noises over-head, which disturbed the dignity and repose of the tea party.

And I think that some day I shall have to make another, larger, book, to tell you more about Tom Kitten!

As for the Puddle-ducks— they went into a pond.

The clothes all came off directly, because there were no buttons.

And Mr. Drake Puddle-duck, and Jemima and Rebeccah, have been looking for them ever since.

THE END

THE TALE OF
JEMIMA
PUDDLE-DUCK

1908

ABOUT THIS BOOK

Beatrix Potter's love of Hill Top and farming shine through this story. She painted her farm manager's wife, Mrs. Cannon, feeding the poultry, while the children Ralph and Betsy (to whom this "farmyard tale" is dedicated) are also illustrated. Kep the collie was Beatrix's favourite sheepdog, and Jemima herself was a real duck who lived at Hill Top. She is a most popular character: self-important, naive, but very endearing.

The story also contains many delightful views of Sawrey: Jemima's wood can still be seen, the view from the hills above the farm, across Esthwaite Water, has not changed, and the Tower Bank Arms is still the local village pub. This blend of fantasy and reality, so often to be found in Beatrix Potter's work, gives a ring of truth to her imaginary world.

WHAT a funny sight it is to see a brood of duck-lings with a hen!
—Listen to the story of Jemima Puddle-duck, who was annoyed because the farmer's wife would not let her hatch her own eggs.

Her sister-in-law, Mrs. Rebeccah Puddle-duck, was perfectly willing to leave the hatching to someone else—"I have not the patience to sit on a nest for twenty-eight days; and no more have you, Jemima. You would let them go cold; you know you would!"

"I wish to hatch my own eggs; I will hatch them all by myself," quacked Jemima Puddle-duck.

She tried to hide her eggs; but they were always found and carried off.

Jemima Puddle-duck became quite desperate. She determined to make a nest right away from the farm.

She set off on a fine spring afternoon along the cart-road that leads over the hill.

She was wearing a shawl and a poke bonnet.

When she reached the top of the hill, she saw a wood in the distance.

She thought that it looked a safe quiet spot.

Jemima Puddle-duck was not much in the habit of flying. She ran downhill a few yards flapping her shawl, and then she jumped off into the air.

She flew beautifully when she had got a good start.

She skimmed along over the tree-tops until she saw an open place in the middle of the wood, where the trees and brushwood had been cleared.

Jemima alighted rather heavily, and began to waddle about in search of a convenient dry nesting-place.

She rather fancied a tree-stump amongst some tall fox-gloves.

But—seated upon the stump, she was startled to find an elegantly dressed gentleman reading a newspaper.

He had black prick ears and sandy-coloured whiskers.

"Quack?" said Jemima Puddle-duck, with her head and her bonnet on one side— "Quack?"

The gentleman raised his eyes above his newspaper and looked curiously at Jemima—

"Madam, have you lost your way?" said he. He had a long bushy tail which he was sitting upon, as the stump was somewhat damp.

Jemima thought him mighty civil and handsome. She explained that she had not lost her way, but that she was trying to find a convenient dry nesting-place.

"Ah! Is that so? Indeed!" said the gentleman with sandy whiskers, looking curiously at Jemima. He folded up the newspaper, and put it in his coat-tail pocket.

Jemima complained of the superfluous hen.

"Indeed! How interesting!

I wish I could meet with that fowl. I would teach it to mind its own business!

"But as to a nest—there is no difficulty: I have a sackful of feathers in my woodshed. No, my dear madam, you will be in nobody's way. You may sit there as long as you like," said the bushy long-tailed gentleman.

He led the way to a very retired, dismal-looking house amongst the fox-gloves.

It was built of faggots and turf, and there were two broken pails, one on top of another, by way of a chimney.

"This is my summer residence; you would not find my earth—my winter house— so convenient," said the hospitable gentleman.

There was a tumble-down shed at the back of the house, made of old soap-boxes. The gentleman opened the door, and showed Jemima in.

The shed was almost quite full of feathers—it was almost suffocating; but it was comfortable and very soft.

Jemima Puddle-duck was rather surprised to find such a vast quantity of feathers. But it was very comfortable; and she made a nest without any trouble at all.

When she came out, the sandy-whiskered gentleman was sitting on a log reading the newspaper—at least he had it spread out, but he was looking over the top of it.

He was so polite, that he seemed almost sorry to let Jemima go home for the night. He promised to take great care of her nest until she came back again next day.

He said he loved eggs and ducklings; he should be proud to see a fine nestful in his wood-shed.

Jemima Puddle-duck came every afternoon; she laid nine eggs in the nest. They were greeny white and very large. The

foxy gentleman admired them immensely. He used to turn them over and count them when Jemima was not there.

At last Jemima told him that she intended to begin to sit next day—"and I will bring a bag of corn with me, so that I need never leave my nest until the eggs are hatched. They might catch cold," said the conscientious Jemima.

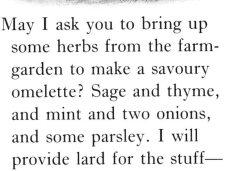

"Madam, I beg you not to trouble yourself with a bag; I will provide oats. But before you commence your tedious sitting, I intend to give you a treat. Let us have a dinner-party all to ourselves! May I ask you to bring up some herbs from the farm-garden to make a savoury omelette? Sage and thyme, and mint and two onions, and some parsley. I will provide lard for the stuff—

lard for the omelette," said the hospitable gentleman with sandy whiskers.

Jemima Puddle-duck was a simpleton: not even the mention of sage and onions made her suspicious.

She went round the farm-garden, nibbling off snippets of all the different sorts of herbs that are used for stuffing roast duck.

And she waddled into the kitchen, and got two onions out of a basket.

The collie-dog Kep met her coming out. "What are you doing with those onions? Where do you go every after-noon by yourself, Jemima Puddle-duck?"

Jemima was rather in awe of the collie; she told him the whole story.

The collie listened, with his wise head on one side; he grinned when she described the polite gentleman with sandy whiskers.

He asked several questions about the wood, and about the exact position of the house and shed.

Then he went out, and trotted down the village. He went to look for two fox-hound puppies who were out at walk with the butcher.

Jemima Puddle-duck went up the cart-road for the last time, on a sunny afternoon. She was rather burdened with bunches of herbs and two onions in a bag.

She flew over the wood, and alighted opposite the house of the bushy long-tailed gentleman.

He was sitting on a log; he sniffed the air, and kept glancing uneasily round the wood. When Jemima alighted he quite jumped.

"Come into the house as soon as you have looked at your eggs. Give me the herbs for the omelette. Be sharp!"

He was rather abrupt. Jemima Puddle-duck had never heard him speak like that.

She felt surprised, and uncomfortable.

While she was inside she heard pattering feet round the back of the shed. Some-one with a black nose sniffed at the bottom of the door, and then locked it.

Jemima became much alarmed.

A moment afterwards there were most awful noises—barking, baying, growls and howls, squealing and groans.

And nothing more was ever seen of that foxy-whiskered gentleman.

Presently Kep opened the door of the shed, and let out Jemima Puddle-duck.

Unfortunately the puppies rushed in and gobbled up all the eggs before he could stop them.

He had a bite on his ear and both the puppies were limping. Jemima Puddle-duck was escorted home in tears on account of those eggs.

She laid some more in June, and she was permitted to keep them herself: but only four of them hatched.

Jemima Puddle-duck said that it was because of her nerves; but she had always been a bad sitter.

THE END

THE TALE OF
JOHNNY
TOWN-MOUSE

1918

ABOUT THIS BOOK

The Tale of Johnny Town-Mouse is set in Lake District surroundings: Johnny lives in the town of Hawkshead, as one can tell from the archway in one of the pictures, while Timmy Willie has his home in a Sawrey garden. Old Diamond, Beatrix's farm horse, pulls the carrier's cart (her favourite of all the pictures), and the cook is a local woman, Mrs. Rogerson. Johnny Town-mouse himself is based on a Doctor Parsons, who would bring his long bag of clubs (drawn in the cover picture on the previous page) to play golf with Beatrix's husband, Willie Heelis.

The theme of the tale is taken from a fable by Aesop, and Beatrix dedicated the story to "Aesop in the shadows." Her sight was failing, and she despaired of the drawings. "I *cannot* see to put colour in them." However the country pictures, in particular, are as delightful as ever.

JOHNNY TOWN-MOUSE was born in a cupboard. Timmy Willie was born in a garden. Timmy Willie was a little country mouse who went to town by mistake in a hamper. The gardener sent vegetables to town once a week by carrier; he packed them in a big hamper.

The gardener left the hamper by the garden gate, so that the carrier could pick it up when he passed. Timmy Willie crept in through a hole in the wickerwork, and after eating some peas— Timmy Willie fell fast asleep.

He awoke in a fright, while the hamper was being lifted into the carrier's cart. Then there was a jolting, and a clattering of horse's feet; other packages were thrown in; for miles and miles —jolt—jolt—jolt! and Timmy Willie trembled amongst the jumbled-up vegetables.

At last the cart stopped at a house, where the hamper was taken out, carried in, and set down. The cook gave the carrier sixpence; the back door banged, and the cart rumbled away. But there was no quiet; there seemed to be hundreds of carts passing. Dogs barked; boys whistled in the street; the cook laughed, the parlour maid ran up and down-stairs; and a canary sang like a steam engine.

Timmy Willie, who had lived all his life in a garden, was almost frightened to death. Presently the cook opened the hamper and began to unpack the vegetables. Out sprang the terrified Timmy Willie.

Up jumped the cook on a chair, exclaiming "A mouse! A mouse! Call the cat! Fetch me the poker, Sarah!" Timmy Willie did not wait for Sarah with the poker; he rushed along the skirting board till he came to a little hole, and in he popped.

He dropped half a foot, and crashed into the middle of a mouse dinner party, breaking three glasses.—"Who in the world is this?" inquired Johnny Town-mouse. But after the first exclamation of surprise he instantly recovered his manners.

With the utmost politeness he introduced Timmy Willie to nine other mice, all with long tails and white neck-ties. Timmy Willie's own tail was insignificant. Johnny Town-mouse and his friends noticed it; but they were too well bred to make personal remarks; only one of them asked Timmy Willie if he had ever been in a trap?

The dinner was of eight courses; not much of anything, but truly elegant. All the dishes were unknown to Timmy Willie, who would have been a little afraid of tasting them; only he was very hungry, and very anxious to behave with company manners.

The continual noise upstairs made him so nervous, that he dropped a plate. "Never mind, they don't belong to us," said Johnny.

"Why don't those youngsters come back with the dessert?" It should be explained that two young mice, who were waiting on the others, went skirmishing upstairs to the kitchen between courses. Several times they had come tumbling in, squeaking and laughing; Timmy Willie learnt with horror that they were being chased by the cat. His appetite failed, he felt faint. "Try some jelly?" said Johnny Town-mouse.

"No? Would you rather go to bed? I will show you a most comfortable sofa pillow."

The sofa pillow had a hole in it. Johnny Town-mouse quite honestly recommended it as the best bed, kept exclusively for visitors. But the sofa smelt of cat. Timmy Willie preferred to spend a miserable night under the fender.

It was just the same next day. An excellent breakfast was provided—for mice accustomed to eat bacon; but Timmy Willie had been reared on roots and salad. Johnny Town-mouse and his friends racketted about under the floors, and came boldly out all over the house in the evening. One particularly loud crash had been caused by Sarah tumbling downstairs with the tea-tray; there were crumbs and sugar and smears of jam to be collected, in spite of the cat.

Timmy Willie longed to be at home in his peaceful nest in a sunny bank. The food disagreed with him; the noise prevented him from sleeping. In a few days he grew so thin that Johnny Town-mouse noticed it, and questioned him. He listened to Timmy Willie's story and inquired about the garden. "It sounds rather a dull place? What do you do when it rains?"

"When it rains, I sit in my little sandy burrow and shell corn and seeds from my Autumn store. I peep out at the throstles and blackbirds on the lawn, and my friend Cock Robin. And when the sun comes out again, you should see my garden and the flowers—roses and pinks and pansies—no noise except the birds and bees, and the lambs in the meadows."

"There goes that cat again!" exclaimed Johnny Town-mouse. When they had taken refuge in the coal-cellar he resumed the conversation: "I confess I am a little disappointed; we have endeavoured to entertain you, Timothy William."

"Oh yes, yes, you have been most kind; but I do feel so ill," said Timmy Willie.

"It may be that your teeth and digestion are unaccustomed to our food; perhaps it might be wiser for you to return in the hamper."

"Oh? Oh!" cried Timmy Willie.

"Why of course for the matter of that we could have sent you back last week," said Johnny rather huffily—"Did you not know that the hamper goes back empty on Saturdays?"

So Timmy Willie said good-bye to his new friends, and hid in the hamper with a crumb of cake and a withered cabbage leaf; and after much jolting, he was set down safely in his own garden.

Sometimes on Saturdays he went to look at the hamper lying by the gate, but he knew better than to get in again. And nobody got out, though Johnny Town-mouse had half promised a visit.

The winter passed; the sun came out again; Timmy Willie sat by his burrow warming his little fur coat and sniffing the smell of violets and spring grass.

He had nearly forgotten his visit to town. When up the sandy path all spick and span with a brown leather bag came Johnny Town-mouse!

Timmy Willie received him with open arms. "You have come at the best of all the year, we will have herb pudding and sit in the sun."

"H'm'm! It is a little damp," said Johnny Town-mouse, who was carrying his tail under his arm, out of the mud.

"What is that fearful noise?" he started violently.

"That?" said Timmy Willie. "That is only a cow; I will beg a little milk, they are quite harmless, unless they happen to lie down upon you. How are all our friends?"

Johnny's account was rather middling. He explained why he was paying his visit so early in the season; the family had gone to the sea-side for Easter; the cook was doing spring cleaning, on board wages, with particular instructions to clear out the mice. There were four kittens, and the cat had killed the canary.

"They say we did it; but I know better," said Johnny Town-mouse. "Whatever is that fearful racket?"

"That is only the lawn-mower; I will fetch some of the grass clippings presently to make your bed. I am sure you had better settle in the country, Johnny."

"H'm'm—we shall see by Tuesday week; the hamper is stopped while they are at the sea-side."

"I am sure you will never want to live in town again," said Timmy Willie.

But he did. He went back in the very next hamper of vegetables; he said it was too quiet!!

One place suits one person, another place suits another person. For my part I prefer to live in the country, like Timmy Willie.

THE END

The Tale of
The Pie
and The Patty-Pan

1905

ABOUT THIS BOOK

This story is rooted very firmly in the village of Sawrey, though Beatrix Potter was not yet living there when she sketched its lanes, houses and gardens in 1902. It was originally written in 1903, then laid aside until 1905. The tale reflects Beatrix's affection for the Lake District village and its inhabitants, and was one she was particularly pleased with: "If the book prints well it will be my next favourite to the *Tailor*." It was published in 1905, in a larger size than the other books, being reduced to the standard format in 1930 and listed as the seventeenth of *The Original Peter Rabbit Books*. The dedication reads, "For Joan [one of the Moore daughters], to read to Baby" [Beatrix's god-daughter, named after her, born in November 1903].

ONCE upon a time there was a Pussy-cat called Ribby, who invited a little dog called Duchess, to tea.

"Come in good time, my dear Duchess," said Ribby's letter, "and we will have something so very nice. I am baking it in a pie-dish—a pie-dish with a pink rim. You never tasted anything so good! And *you* shall eat it all! *I* will eat muffins, my dear Duchess!" wrote Ribby.

Duchess read the letter and wrote an answer:—"I will come with much pleasure at a quarter past four. But it is very strange. *I* was just going to invite you to come here, to supper, my dear Ribby, to eat something *most delicious.*

"I will come very punctually, my dear Ribby," wrote Duchess; and then at the end she added—"I hope it isn't mouse?"

And then she thought that did not look quite polite; so she scratched out "isn't mouse" and changed it to "I hope it will be fine," and she gave her letter to the postman.

But she thought a great deal about Ribby's pie, and she read Ribby's letter over and over again.

"I am dreadfully afraid it *will* be mouse!" said Duchess to herself—"I really couldn't, *couldn't* eat mouse pie. And I shall have to eat it, because it is a party. And *my* pie was going to be veal and ham. A pink and white pie-dish! and so is mine; just like Ribby's dishes; they were both bought at Tabitha Twitchit's."

Duchess went into her larder and took the pie off a shelf and looked at it.

"It is all ready to put into the oven. Such lovely pie-crust; and I put in a little tin patty-pan to hold up the crust; and I made a hole in the middle with a fork to let out the steam— Oh I do wish I could eat my own pie, instead of a pie made of mouse!"

Duchess considered and considered and read Ribby's letter again—

"A pink and white pie-dish—and *you* shall eat it *all*. 'You' means me—then Ribby is not going to even taste the pie herself? A pink and white pie-dish! Ribby is sure to go out to buy the muffins . . . Oh what a good idea! Why shouldn't I rush along and put my pie into Ribby's oven when Ribby isn't there?"

Duchess was quite delighted with her own cleverness!

Ribby in the meantime had received Duchess's answer, and as soon as she was sure that the little dog could come—she popped

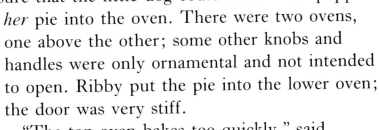

her pie into the oven. There were two ovens, one above the other; some other knobs and handles were only ornamental and not intended to open. Ribby put the pie into the lower oven; the door was very stiff.

"The top oven bakes too quickly," said Ribby to herself. "It is a pie of the most delicate and tender mouse minced up with bacon. And I have taken out all the bones;

because Duchess did nearly choke herself with a fish-bone last time I gave a party. She eats a little fast—rather big mouthfuls. But a most genteel and elegant little dog; infinitely superior company to Cousin Tabitha Twitchit."

Ribby put on some coal and swept up the hearth. Then she went out with a can to the well, for water to fill up the kettle.

Then she began to set the room in order, for it was the sitting-room as well as the kitchen. She shook the mats out at the front door and put them straight; the hearth-rug was a rabbit-skin. She dusted the clock and the ornaments on the mantel-piece, and she polished and rubbed the tables and chairs.

Then she spread a very clean white table-cloth, and set out her best china tea-set, which she took out of a wall-cupboard near the fireplace.

The tea-cups were white with a pattern of pink roses; and the dinner-plates were white and blue.

When Ribby had laid the table she took a jug and a blue and white dish, and went out down the field to the farm, to fetch milk and butter.

When she came back, she peeped into the bottom oven; the pie looked very comfortable.

Ribby put on her shawl and bonnet and went out again with a basket, to the village

shop to buy a packet of tea, a pound of lump sugar, and a pot of marmalade.

And just at the same time, Duchess came out of *her* house, at the other end of the village.

Ribby met Duchess half-way down the street, also carrying a basket, covered with a cloth. They only bowed to one another;

they did not speak, because they were going to have a party.

As soon as Duchess had got round the corner out of sight—she simply ran! Straight away to Ribby's house!

Ribby went into the shop and bought what she required, and came out, after a pleasant gossip with Cousin Tabitha Twitchit.

Cousin Tabitha was disdainful afterwards in conversation—

"A little *dog* indeed! Just as if there were no CATS in Sawrey! And a *pie* for afternoon tea! The very idea!" said Cousin Tabitha Twitchit.

Ribby went on to Timothy Baker's and bought the muffins. Then she went home.

There seemed to be a sort of scuffling noise in the back passage, as she was coming in at the front door.

"I trust that is not that Pie: the spoons are locked up, however," said Ribby.

But there was nobody there. Ribby opened the bottom oven door with some difficulty, and turned the pie. There began to be a pleasing smell of baked mouse!

Duchess in the meantime, had slipped out at the back door.

"It is a very odd thing that Ribby's pie was *not* in the oven when I put mine in! And I can't find it anywhere; I have looked all over the house. I put *my* pie into a nice hot oven at the top. I could not turn any of the other handles; I think that they are all shams," said Duchess, "but I wish I could have removed the pie made of mouse! I cannot think what she has done with it? I heard Ribby coming and I had to run out by the back door!"

Duchess went home and brushed her beautiful black coat; and then she picked a bunch of flowers in her garden as a present for Ribby; and passed the time until the clock struck four.

Ribby—having assured herself by careful search that there was really no one hiding in the cupboard or in the larder—went upstairs to change her dress.

She put on a lilac silk gown, for the party, and an embroidered muslin apron and tippet.

"It is very strange," said Ribby, "I did not *think* I left that drawer pulled out; has some-body been trying on my mittens?"

She came downstairs again, and made the tea, and put the teapot on the hob. She peeped again into the *bottom* oven, the pie had become a lovely brown, and it was steaming hot.

She sat down before the fire to wait for the little dog. "I am glad I used the *bottom* oven," said Ribby, "the top one would certainly have been very much too hot. I wonder why that cupboard door was open? Can there really have been someone in the house?"

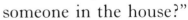

Very punctually at four o'clock, Duchess started to go to the party. She ran so fast through the village that she was too early, and she had to wait a little while in the

lane that leads down to Ribby's house.

"I wonder if Ribby has taken *my* pie out of the oven yet?" said Duchess, "and whatever can have become of the other pie made of mouse?"

At a quarter past four to the minute, there came a most genteel little tap-tappity. "Is Mrs. Ribston at home?" inquired Duchess in the porch.

"Come in! and how do you do, my dear Duchess?" cried

Ribby. "I hope I see you well?"

"Quite well, I thank you, and how do *you* do, my dear Ribby?" said Duchess. "I've brought you some flowers; what a delicious smell of pie!"

"Oh, what lovely flowers! Yes, it is mouse and bacon!"

"Do not talk about food, my dear Ribby," said Duchess; "what a lovely white tea-cloth! . . . Is it done to a turn? Is it still in the oven?"

"I think it wants another five minutes," said Ribby. "Just a shade longer; I will pour out the tea, while we wait. Do you take sugar, my dear Duchess?"

"Oh yes, please! my dear Ribby; and may I have a lump upon my nose?"

"With pleasure, my dear Duchess; how beautifully you beg! Oh, how sweetly pretty!"

Duchess sat up with the sugar on her nose and sniffed—

"How good that pie smells! I do love veal and ham—I mean to say mouse and bacon—"

She dropped the sugar in confusion, and had to go hunting under the tea-table, so did not see which oven Ribby opened in order to get out the pie.

Ribby set the pie upon the table; there was a very savoury smell.

Duchess came out from under the table-cloth munching sugar, and sat up on a chair.

"I will first cut the pie for you; I am going to have muffin and marmalade," said Ribby.

"Do you really prefer muffin? Mind the patty-pan!"

"I beg your pardon?" said Ribby.

"May I pass you the marmalade?" said Duchess hurriedly.

The pie proved extremely toothsome, and the muffins light and hot. They disappeared rapidly, especially the pie!

"I think"—(thought the Duchess to herself)—"I *think* it would be wiser if I helped myself to pie; though Ribby did not seem to notice anything when she was cutting it. What very small fine pieces it has cooked into! I did not remember that I had minced it up so fine; I suppose this is a quicker oven than my own."

"How fast Duchess is eating!" thought Ribby to herself, as she buttered her fifth muffin.

The pie-dish was emptying rapidly! Duchess had had four helps already, and was fumbling with the spoon.

"A little more bacon, my dear Duchess?" said Ribby.

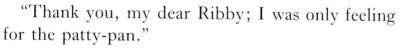

"Thank you, my dear Ribby; I was only feeling for the patty-pan."

"The patty-pan? my dear Duchess?"

"The patty-pan that held up the pie-crust," said Duchess, blushing under her black coat.

"Oh, I didn't put one in, my dear Duchess," said Ribby; "I don't think that it is necessary in pies made of mouse."

Duchess fumbled with the spoon—"I can't find it!" she said anxiously.

"There isn't a patty-pan," said Ribby, looking perplexed.

"Yes, indeed, my dear Ribby; where can it have gone to?" said Duchess.

"There most certainly is not one, my dear Duchess. I disapprove of tin articles in puddings and pies. It is most

undesirable—(especially when people swallow in lumps!)" she added in a lower voice.

Duchess looked very much alarmed, and continued to scoop the inside of the pie-dish.

"My Great-aunt Squintina (grandmother of Cousin Tabitha Twitchit) —died of a thimble in a Christmas plum-pudding. *I* never put any article of metal in *my* puddings or pies."

Duchess looked aghast, and tilted up the pie-dish.

"I have only four patty-pans, and they are all in the cupboard."

Duchess set up a howl.

"I shall die! I shall die! I have swallowed a patty-pan! Oh, my dear Ribby, I do feel so ill!"

"It is impossible, my dear Duchess; there was not a patty-pan."

Duchess moaned and whined and rocked herself about.

"Oh I feel so dreadful, I have swallowed a patty-pan!"

"There was *nothing* in the pie," said Ribby severely.

"Yes there *was,* my dear Ribby, I am sure I have swallowed it!"

"Let me prop you up with a pillow, my dear Duchess; where do you think you feel it?"

"Oh I do feel so ill *all over* me, my dear Ribby; I have swallowed a large tin patty-pan with a sharp scalloped edge!"

"Shall I run for the doctor? I will just lock up the spoons!"

"Oh yes, yes! fetch Dr. Maggotty, my dear Ribby: he is a Pie himself, he will certainly understand."

Ribby settled Duchess in an armchair before the fire, and went out and hurried to the village to look for the doctor.

She found him at the smithy.

He was occupied in putting rusty nails into a bottle of ink, which he had obtained at the post office.

"Gammon? ha! HA!" said he, with his head on one side.

Ribby explained that her guest had swallowed a patty-pan.

"Spinach? ha! HA!" said he, and accompanied her with alacrity.

He hopped so fast that Ribby had to run. It was most conspicuous. All the village could see that Ribby was fetching the doctor.

"I *knew* that they would over-eat themselves!" said Cousin Tabitha Twitchit.

But while Ribby had been hunting for the doctor—a curious thing had happened to Duchess, who had been left by herself, sitting before the fire, sighing and groaning and feeling very unhappy.

"How *could* I have swallowed it! such a large thing as a patty-pan!"

She got up and went to the table, and felt inside the pie-dish again with a spoon.

"No; there is no patty-pan, and I put one in; and nobody has eaten pie except me, so I must have swallowed it!"

She sat down again, and stared mournfully at the grate. The fire crackled and danced, and something sizz-z-zled!

Duchess started! She opened the door of the *top* oven;—out came a rich steamy flavour of veal and ham, and there stood a fine brown pie,—and through a hole in the top of the pie-crust there was a glimpse of a little tin patty-pan!

Duchess drew a long breath—

"Then I must have been eating MOUSE! . . . No wonder I feel ill . . . But perhaps I should feel worse if I had really swallowed a patty-pan!" Duchess reflected—"What a very awkward thing to have to explain to Ribby! I think I will put *my* pie in the back-yard and say nothing about it. When I go home, I will run round and take it away." She put it outside

the back-door, and sat down again by the fire, and shut her eyes; when Ribby arrived with the doctor, she seemed fast asleep.

"Gammon, ha, HA?" said the doctor.

"I am feeling very much better," said Duchess, waking up with a jump.

"I am truly glad to hear it! He has brought you a pill, my dear Duchess!"

"I think I should feel *quite* well if he only felt my pulse," said Duchess, backing away from the magpie, who sidled up with something in his beak.

"It is only a bread pill, you had much better take it; drink a little milk, my dear Duchess!"

"Gammon? Gammon?" said the doctor, while Duchess coughed and choked.

"Don't say that again!" said Ribby, losing her temper—"Here, take this bread and jam, and get out into the yard!"

"Gammon and Spinach! ha ha HA!" shouted Dr. Maggotty triumphantly outside the back door.

"I am feeling very much better my dear Ribby," said Duchess. "Do you not think that I had better go home before it gets dark?"

"Perhaps it might be wise, my dear Duchess. I will lend you a nice warm shawl, and you shall take my arm."

"I would not trouble you for worlds; I feel wonderfully better. One pill of Dr. Maggotty—"

"Indeed it is most admirable, if it has cured you of a patty-pan! I will call directly after breakfast to ask how you have slept."

Ribby and Duchess said goodbye affectionately, and Duchess started home. Half-way up the lane she stopped and looked back; Ribby had gone in and shut her door. Duchess slipped through the fence, and ran round to the back of Ribby's house, and peeped into the yard.

Upon the roof of the pig-stye sat Dr. Maggotty and three jackdaws. The jackdaws were eating pie-crust, and the magpie was drinking gravy out of a patty-pan.

"Gammon, ha, HA!" he shouted when he saw Duchess's little black nose peeping round the corner.

Duchess ran home feeling uncommonly silly!

When Ribby came out for a pailful of water to wash up the tea-things, she found a pink and white pie-dish lying smashed in the middle of the yard. The patty-pan was under the pump, where Dr. Maggotty had considerately left it.

Ribby stared with amazement—"Did you ever see the like! So there really *was* a patty-pan? . . . But *my* patty-pans are all in the kitchen cupboard. Well I never did! . . . Next time I want to give a party—I will invite Cousin Tabitha Twitchit!"

THE END

NATIONS
OF THE
WORLD